CATS

A COLLECTION OF HEARTWARMING FURRY-TALES

volume 3

KATHRYN JANE

CATS: A Collection of Heartwarming Furry-Tales, Volume 3
By: Kathryn Jane
Cover by The Killion Group
ISBN: 978-988790-00-8

kathrynjane.com

Other books by Kathryn Jane

CATS Volume 1
CATS Volume 2
CATS Volume 3

INTO THE SUNRISE

INTREPID WOMEN SERIES
Book 1 – Do Not Tell Me No
Book 2 – Touch Me
Book 3 – Daring To Love
Book 4 – Voices
Book 5 – Lies
Book 6 – All She Wanted
Book 7 – Dance With Me

CONTENTS

KATHRYN JANE

ACKNOWLEDGMENTS

Without the Killion Group designing my covers,
Demon for Details doing a fabulous job of editing,
Judicious Revisions proofreading and both L. J.
Charles and Barb lending their talents as critiquers,
this book wouldn't look or sound anything like it
does today.
Ladies, I thank you all profusely!

DEDICATION

CATS: Volume 3, is dedicated to all the ferals and barn cats I've known. I loved your tenacity, and sense of humor, and wish I'd been able to save more of you.

CATS: the series, is dedicated to Bear and Wolfe, a one of a kind pair of cats who were with me for the first book I wrote, and almost every one since.

My boys, I hope you're having a wonderful time on the other side of the bridge. Romping in the green grass and up the cedar trees, then sleeping off your fun while snoozing in warm sun puddles.

1

PEEP

Tony studied the tiny cat dancing her way across the rooftops of several outbuildings. Ginger stripes and a stubby tail made her cute, but it was her smart choices that impressed him.

In the few days since her arrival, she'd kept her distance from the others, only approaching the feeding station when it was unoccupied. And she stayed up high, rarely setting foot on the ground.

With more savvy than the average newcomer, she was sure to be one of the rare survivors.

Tony hadn't seen many like this in his years of mentoring newcomers. Dumped housecats rarely had any idea how to survive on their own outdoors. There *had* been major successes over the years with cats like Zak, who took to ranch life as if he'd been born here, but also many heartbreaking losses. It was discouraging when warnings and lessons went unheeded and lovely cats full of life were snatched up by predators.

Tony had moved to a different level now, and Zak was now the colony's mentor, but still, this newbie tugged on him. Perhaps he'd make her a special project. He *was* allowed one occasionally.

The tiny ginger had a way about her that made him smile inside, and he just couldn't resist, so he made himself visible and stepped into her path.

She backed up a few steps, deliberately lowering to a sitting position.

Welcome.

She slow blinked.

I'm Tony.

Recognition flickered in her eyes. *You're the leader of the colony. The others describe you as a massive tabby with a crinkled ear and a crooked smile.*

Old war wounds. He hesitated while considering the rest of his reply, uncertain why he wasn't ready to tell her the truth. *I'm not exactly the leader these days.*

They respect you.

We respect each other. He was quite taken by the directness of her golden gaze.

My name is Peep, and I'm happy to meet you.

That's an unusual name.

My meow is broken, or I never had one, and the only sound I can make is "peep," so the children called me that.

Children. I see. You had people, yet you have a great sense of self-preservation, like a feral.

I was born in the hayloft at a boarding stable. Mamma taught us to stay up high so we'd be safe when people brought their dogs with them.

Sounds like a good home. How did you end up here?

The stable was sold, and the barn was to be demolished. We were all trapped and fixed, and then there was a place where we were taken so we could get new homes. She sighed.

The cages made loud noises, and people got very close to stare in and talk and poke, and I hated every minute.

It must have been very hard.

Only for me, I guess. Many of my friends and family liked it, and tried to convince me to stop hiding.

But you didn't.

Couldn't. One day someone came asking for barn cats, and they were brought to my cage. Next thing I knew, I was in a crate, in a truck, and when it stopped, the crate was opened, and I was here.

This is a good place. There's always food for us in the loft, and lots of mice in the hay. And the people who come here are kind.

I don't mind people, as long as they don't try to hold on to me.

Do you like being petted?

Sometimes.

The lady who fills the feed barrel every few weeks likes to sit in the hay to talk to us. She has special treats for those willing to be petted, and anyone who will sit in her lap gets lots of them.

I'll watch for her.

You'll know when she's here, since all the cats get excited and go running because she brings the special cans of food.

I liked food from a can when they brought it every morning at the shelter.

Sometimes she brings toona, too. But in the meantime, the barrel always has kibble for us. It never runs out.

That's quite wonderful. The barn where I used to live had big dishes that sometimes got empty.

It had been less than a year since the lady used a rope to lift the big plastic barrel up into the loft. Then she dragged up huge bags of kibble to dump into it, and the cats all gathered to eat from where it spilled out of small triangles cut out of the bottom. She stood by and told them how she'd designed it so four cats could eat at the same time without bothering each other. And how they'd never have to worry about food, even if there was a blizzard and she couldn't get here for a week.

It's called a gravity feeder, whatever that means. He remembered one of the cats calling it magic, and it *was* quite wonderful. Years of not knowing where he'd find his next meal were now distant memories. *Sometimes other creatures like raccoons come by for a snack, too.*

Peep yawned. Had he been preaching? Boring her? *Is there anything you'd like to know about living here?*

She wandered to the edge of the loft and gazed across the barnyard. *Is there a safe time? To be on the ground, I mean. Like when people are here?*

It's never completely safe. A coyote came right up on the porch of the house and snatched a small dog once.

Peep shuddered and glanced toward the house.

CATS

People used to live there?

Up until the fire. Then there was an auction, and now the lady who feeds us is fixing it up so she can live there someday. She does hammering and stuff inside, and a man comes to work on it too. Brings a big old black dog with him.

Sometimes dogs where I lived chased the cats.

No worries with this guy, he's very kind. Likes to hang out with us while the man works.

That's cool. What's with that big white creature who hangs with the goats? He's always staring at me.

Name's Elliott. What they call a guardian llama. If you stick close to him, you can safely cross the barnyard on the ground. Coyotes won't mess with him, and even the barn owls give him a wide berth.

Tony yawned. Must have caught it from her, or all this talk was making him sleepy. *Come, I'll show you one of the best spots for day-napping.*

He led her to the very top of the stack of hay at the far end of the loft, went across to the middle and dropped into an opening which led to a tunnel between bales. The convoluted journey was well worth the destination—a patch of sunshine just big enough for two cats to stretch out and soak up rays.

Tony made himself comfortable.

Peep would have loved to snuggle in close beside him, longed to feel the warmth of another cat, the vibration of a purr, but he'd left her lots of room, which likely meant he wasn't inviting closeness. Besides, she'd been a loner for so long, it would be hard to allow herself the luxury of such a comfort. Perhaps one day.

In the meantime, Tony's friendship, and sharing his special place, made her heart sigh, and she drifted off to sleep happier than ever before.

Life was very pleasant for several weeks, while Peep settled into the way things worked at the ranch. Sometimes nothing happened at all, and a day could be spent watching flies zip around. Or checking out the other animals.

Peep liked watching the goats while they very carefully selected which tiny weed or blade of grass to eat next. And the baby cows were hilarious when they romped and played and butted heads. It was odd when the mamma cows left them hidden in the tall grass and went off to graze in the fields far away.

The horses weren't as friendly as the ones where Peep came from, and mostly grazed far from the barn, where the grass was lush. But then there was Dickens, the donkey. He liked everyone, apparently, and was a busy fellow, always up to something. He even knew how to get across the cattle guard, like the goats did, so he roamed wherever he pleased.

Peep, too, liked to roam, and went on daily wanders over the buildings, along the fence lines, and occasionally perched on the roof of the woodshed to watch the goings-on.

One day, when she hopped up on the shed, she looked down into the yard behind the house and saw a terrible sight—Elliott, the llama, spread out on the grass like he'd been shot dead. Peep couldn't see any blood, but she was positive he wasn't breathing.

She took off at a run, flew all the way back to the barn, shouting for Tony, couldn't find him anywhere, and then suddenly he was right in front of her.

What's wrong?

It's Elliott. I think he's dead!

Tony got a funny look on his face. *Is he sprawled out on the grass somewhere?*

Yes! How did you know?

Probably sleeping.

But he wasn't breathing!

He takes breaks sometimes. Come on. I'll show you.

On the way back, Peep had to stop several times to wait for Tony, and was getting frustrated at his lack of concern, but held her tongue, and scooted on ahead. She was shocked to find Elliott grazing near where he'd been dead. Or looking dead, at least.

She parked her butt and stared. *I don't understand. How could I have been so mistaken?*

It's trickery, Miss Peep.

Startled, she stared at the llama. He'd never spoken to her before.

I take very short naps, and slow my breathing down to almost nothing. It serves to trick the predators who might get ideas about making a move on the goats while I'm sleeping.

That doesn't make sense.

If they think I'm asleep, they'll try to sneak past me, but they are suspicious if they think I'm dead, because, well, how did I get that way, and is there another predator close by? And secondly, if there's a dead llama to snack on, they'll stop right here, and not bother to chase down a noisy goat.

Peep loved the reasoning and where it was going. *And if they approach you, they'll be in trouble, because you'll beat them up.*

You've got it. Playing dead is a guardian tactic.

Elliott was apparently much smarter than he looked. Another fact worth remembering.

Tony led the way back to the loft, and she paid close attention to the route, one she wasn't familiar with.

They crossed the woodshed, dropped down onto the fence, then quick-stepped along it to hop onto a barrel, a shelf, the top edge of a stall, and up to the loft where the cats spent the bulk of their time.

When they weren't napping, Peep hung out with Tony and his best friend, Zak, a sweet old tabby who was the colony's ambassador and welcoming committee of one.

He was a funny guy in a droll sort of way, but he had one enormous weak spot. The lady who brought them food. He adored her. Paced the edge of the loft, meowing at the top of his lungs while she unloaded supplies from her truck.

She'd laugh up at him and toss him special treats. Then, when she finished filling all the wet food dishes and the kibble bin, she'd sit in the hay, and Zak would climb into her lap and purr and purr while she petted him and rubbed his ears. Then he'd start to drool, and that would make her laugh out loud some more.

Peep liked the lady and her gentle hands, and especially liked the way she gave scritches that started at the ears and ended at the tail. Those felt so good. But Peep wasn't ready to do any lap sitting yet. Even though she longed for closeness, she was having trouble taking those last steps.

For now, she had great fun with the toys the lady made for them. They were delightful to toss and chase and pretend with—as though they were prey. Peep loved hunting, but it wasn't safe anywhere except inside the barn, and with plenty of other cats around, she didn't often get a chance at a catch of her own. So the toys were a good distraction to help her work off some of the longing to hunt.

Sometimes, in the quiet of a long afternoon, Tony would tell her stories of when he'd been young and spry and supplied food for much of his colony—which was small until the new road was put in and people started dumping cats out this way.

She loved when he talked about some of the people who would sneak him into the bunkhouse in years gone by, and how he'd once snuggled in with half-wild cattle during a blizzard.

And all the while he was telling stories, he was teaching her about the ranch and how to have a long life here. The best spots to wait out a storm, and the warmest places to hunker down when winter came to blast them with frigid winds and driving snow.

Storytelling often ended with a nap, and almost always Peep woke to find Zak perched on a bale above, as though on guard, which put a warm feeling inside her. She liked him a lot, and felt like someday they'd be great friends, even though he never played with the rest of them at night.

Instead, he sat high up in the rafters with Tony, keeping watch while the younger set had a rollicking good time, zooming around for the sheer joy of running. Chased each other over rooftops. Stalked imaginary prey, and tumbled about, as carefree as leaves in the wind.

Life couldn't be any better. Good food, shelter, friends, and safety. She even enjoyed some lap time with the lady after a while.

Besides all that, she was half in love with Tony, but she feared he was growing tired of her, because he was spending more and more time with Zak instead of her. The two tabbies were, of course, old friends, and had more in common with each other than with her, but still, it niggled at her some days.

Then one night, while the two elders were high above and the youngsters galloped around playing—during a lull in the shenanigans, everything changed.

Sitting on the outer edge of the loft, surveying the barnyard in the light of the full moon, Peep spotted a fat mouse skittering between the workshop and one of the sheds. She stilled instinctively, and with hunter's eyes she tracked her quarry, gauged the distance.

Definitely too high up to jump, but the ladder…

She bellied down and scooted to get into a better position, then peeked over.

The plump mouse was still there.

Heart thumping, Peep worked her way down one wooden rung at a time until she was only a few feet from the ground and within striking range.

Stop!

But Tony—

Don't do it.

Look how fat—

Stop!

She scanned the area. Saw nothing of concern. *I'll share it with you.*

No, you won't.

I—

Will be down a life.

He was old and cautious, but she was fast. She knew she could grab the prey and be back up in the loft before any passing predator even figured out that she was on the ground.

She vibrated with the need to pounce. *Needed* that mouse. Her vision narrowed, locked on the target. Muscles bunched. Ears flattened.

No!

Tony's voice broke her concentration just when there was a sudden flash of movement.

Fast, silent, and deadly, a coyote shot between the buildings and snapped up the mouse. *Her* mouse.

She shuddered.

He'd have had her before her toes even hit the ground. How had she missed him? Not been aware of his presence?

Tony?

You're okay, Peep. And your lesson has been learned.

He sounded funny. She'd upset him. *Tony?*

My duty is done. Goodbye, little one.

What? Wait, Tony, I'm sorry I was so stupid. Please forgive me.

You are forgiven. And I'll never forget you, but it's time for me to go.

Wait! Her voice shook while she backed up to see higher in the hay, to spot where he was, so she could go to him. The ledge was so close behind her she could feel the empty air, but panic was setting in. *Tony!*

She slipped, flailed in midair. *Tony!*

Her feet struck something soft but solid that pushed her hard, and shot her right back up to the loft instead of into the jaws waiting below.

Heart still in her throat, she stared over the side and saw nothing, then ran, searched, called out, but couldn't find her friend. He saved her life. Even though before that moment she had never touched him, she knew it was Tony who'd shoved her back to safety, and she needed to thank him. She needed to see him so she could really feel safe.

She spotted Zak halfway up the haystack. *Where's Tony?*

Gone.

Her heart stuttered. *How can he just be gone?*

Someone else needed him.

I don't understand.

He's a guardian cat.

I know. He watches over everyone. Saved my life just now.

It's more than that. He's not mortal. At least not anymore. The Tony you met was what some call an angel cat.

And there he was, suddenly in front of her.

Tony!

Zak's telling the truth, little one, he said.

But Tony, you have to be real.

I'm very real, but no longer mortal. My ninth life ended several years ago.

Noooo!

I was allowed to show myself to you because you'll one day be the leader of this colony, and I had much information to pass on to you.

Reality was beginning to sink in. She sat. *For the record? I don't like this much.* Little things started to make sense. There'd never been a head bop, a shoulder rub, and she'd never felt warmth coming from him. Not the physical kind, at least. And a real cat couldn't have saved her when she fell tonight.

Reality was setting in, and when that first bit of panic at the thought of losing him wore off, she was surprised there was no horrible weight on her heart. This wasn't like when other friends had died. It was different. Tony was gone, but still with her, in an odd way.

You're right, little one. I will always be here for you.

Only a tiny bit startled by him reading her thoughts, she smiled inside. She had her very own angel.

So you do.

You said others can't see you. Will it be like that for me, too, now?

For the most part, but you'll hear my voice

from time to time.

But if I need you? Need to see that crinkled ear and crooked smile?

I'll oblige you. But someone else needs me right now, so I have to go.

Talk to me whenever you can, okay?

I promise.

His image faded and her heart did a funny bump. *Look after Zak for me.*

She took a deep breath. *I promise.*

She and Zak were quiet for a while, each with their own thoughts, until Peep glanced at the old tabby. *You were his friend for always.*

I still am.

How long have you been here? Zak often talked about living with humans for years before being thrust into ranch life.

Nearly ten years, and never without Tony. He greeted me when I arrived, and showed me the ropes. I was such a greenhorn. I can't tell you how many times he saved my silly neck, and laughed at me because I was such a city boy.

City boy?

I came from a pampered home. Had never spent more than an hour outdoors in my first six years.

He saved my life tonight.

I know.

She stared at the big tabby for a minute, then sighed. *Zak, I need a hug.*

He shuffled over in the hay. *I've shared my nest with no one since Tony died, but I think it's time now, Miss Peep.*

CATS

She crawled in alongside him, and he curled around her, and a warmth—a kind she hadn't felt with Tony—crept into her soul. This was where she belonged.

From the threshold of the rainbow bridge, where he'd just delivered another old friend, Tony watched Peep and Zak curl up together in their hayloft.

He glanced across at the wide meadow, where cats played happily, or simply snoozed in the sun, and thought, *yes, it would be nice to spend a few days here, until I'm needed again.* And there were his friends, trotting across the bridge to meet him. The old ranch dog who'd always shared his snacks with Tony, with a half dozen cats in his wake.

Tony's heart smiled. What a fine way to take a short vacation.

KATHRYN JANE

2

STANLEY

Stanley's heart slammed against his ribs while he watched from the safety of the pile of fence rails until the tractor roared into view. Although he was no longer blindly terrified of the noisy contraption, his body vibrated with readiness.

If they were coming for rails, he'd scoot under the old camper. If they were here for something else, he'd be safe where he was. The people who worked on the ranch had never done him harm— unlike others from his past—but the tractor couldn't be trusted.

Huge wheels bounced through fresh potholes, the engine revved, and the whine of the lowering bucket had him tensed and ready to spring into action. Then there was silence, instant and complete...except for the thud of a man landing two-footed on half-frozen ground.

It had been quite warm for a few days, and sunny to the point Stanley's nose felt a bit sunburned, but this morning things had changed. The sky was filled with heavy, steel-gray clouds looking like they were about to dump more snow— just when Stanley was hoping spring would drive winter away.

Bypassing Stanley's safe haven, the man clomped over to the pile of scrap lumber, picked out several large pieces of wood and tossed them toward the tractor's bucket, where they landed with a loud bang. Next he went to the barrels lined up along the fence. He rapped his knuckles against them all, then tipped one over, rolled it to the tractor, and added it to the wood.

Stanley was just about to draw a relieved breath when footsteps approached the stack of rails.

Crap. Stanley bolted from the end of the pile, raced wide past the scary four-wheeled machine, and dove under the old camper, hiding between the concrete blocks it rested on—not pleased at having to run through the mud instead of choosing a drier path. He could only hope the man would leave *this* shelter alone. Only once had Stanley ever known them to move it, and on that day the tractor had the long metal things instead of the bucket.

"It's okay, cat, I won't bother you." He always sounded nice enough, but not special like the lady. Stanley had almost given in to her quiet voice a few times, but his feral instincts kept him safe from such a foolhardy move.

The man worked his way through the rails. Measuring, then pitching them into one of several new piles, and by the time he was finished, Stanley's home had been decimated.

CATS

Talk about being forced to relocate.

Sure, there were lots of other areas to choose from, and he'd tried a few when he first arrived here from the city, but nothing was as perfect as this. He loved being far away from the barn where a gazillion other cats lived. Sure, it was a trek to get food, but he didn't mind.

In the beginning he'd made camp in the attic above the machine shop, but that only lasted until the day the ladder was pulled down and the man climbed right up.

That time, Stanley made a dive for the darkest corner and held his breath until he was alone again, undiscovered, but one scare like that was enough for him. He spent the day hunting for a new hideout, until he found this isolated yard where supplies were stored.

When the tractor suddenly roared to life and brought Stanley back to the present, he stayed very still, watching until the loaded machine bounced its way out of sight. The man was going to be busy today.

And so was Stanley.

First, he considered the giant heap of scrap wood. While it *looked* like a good option, he'd recently stepped onto a board at the corner and the other end of it lifted up, dislodging a smaller chunk of wood that tumbled noisily down the pile. Definitely not a good shelter, because it could fall apart under the weight of new snow, or a wily coyote.

The wind started to pick up dead leaves and whirl them into the air. He needed to get a move on.

Perhaps…

A few weeks ago, when he was hunting in the ravine and a storm blew in, he'd taken shelter under a rusty old truck—up inside what was left of the engine—and when the snow stopped and the sun beat down on the hood, it was toasty warm in there. Didn't look like sunshine was going to happen today, but the storms here were often short-lived. Heavy wind made drifting a consideration when seeking shelter, and with the truck there would be multiple ways to get out, so he wasn't likely to get snowed in.

Not too far from the barn, either, if he needed to go there for kibble after. He preferred hunting, but sometimes game was scarce when the weather was ugly.

Best to get a move on.

Stanley picked his way toward the gully, avoiding the scattered patches of dirty old snow, and was about halfway to the ancient truck when the first heavy drops of rain startled him. He scooted under the shelter of a tree and shook them off, but was soon wet again. Hmmm. The trees weren't much shelter without their leaves. Should he race across the field to the barn? Probably weren't any coyotes out right now.

He glanced toward the rusty truck. It was much closer, and Stanley didn't believe in wasting energy. Besides, at the barn there were all those cats he didn't know.

Decision made, he walked at first, but was getting wetter by the minute, and didn't care for it at all. Shaking water from his ears and shoving dignity aside, he made a dash for his chosen shelter. Dove underneath, and spent some time getting his jet-black coat in order and cleaning up his white socks before climbing up into the spot he found the last time he was here.

It was quite cozy, even with rain hammering on the metal above him.

Until the thunder rolled.

Stanley hated thunder, because even covering his ears by curling into a tight little ball didn't stop the rumbling from ripping right through him. And it went on, and on and on for what seemed forever, and once the thunder was finished, he fell into a deep, exhausted sleep.

When the light of morning finally showed under the truck and through the crack at the edge of the hood, Stanley wasn't surprised to see a little run of water beneath him, because it was still raining.

The hair on his neck prickled.

Was there a predator nearby?

Even though he was hungry and needed to hunt, he bided his time, just in case. Rested his chin on his paws and tried to think of happier times, all the while keeping an eye on the ground below, watching for the shadow of a coyote.

That's when he noticed the tiny stream of water had widened, and was moving rapidly. Stanley climbed a bit lower to get a closer look, and was stunned when the water seemed to explode, and suddenly covered the entire area below him. At first he shot higher inside the engine to escape, but his instincts screamed at him to get out before he was completely trapped.

He went to the side opposite where the river had first grown, then dropped down into it.

The first shock was when his feet didn't touch the ground. The second was suddenly being thrust down the center of the gulley in a raging torrent.

Swim!

He paddled hard. Toes spread wide and muscles straining, Stanley aimed for the land alongside the water, but the grip of the brutal current held him captive until he bumped into something solid.

Grabbing frantically at what turned out to be a branch, he fought to hang on while water flew past, rising higher and higher on the bank, until his branch was so far below the surface water washed over his head. He stuck his nose straight up, and his ears filled, then his nostrils, and he had to let go.

Once again at the mercy of the raging current, but not willing to give in, Stanley blinked furiously to clear the water from his eyes and locked on to the sight of a row of low-hanging limbs downstream.

He paddled hard to get out of the central current. Took aim.

Missed.

Tried again.

And again.

And at last it worked. How he got that grip, he'd never know, but he dragged himself up and along the life-saving limb until he reached the safety of the broad tree trunk. He'd just stay there, he thought, but realized the tree would soon be in the middle of the newly born river.

Without hesitation, he made a leap for dry

ground before there wasn't any. Not that where he landed was dry. In fact, the rain made the dusty earth between old bits of ice so slick he slid about ten feet before coming to a stop and picking himself up.

He'd have laughed at the absurdity, or at least celebrated success, if the rest of his journey didn't look so terrifying.

Staring hard through the now-pounding rain, his heart sank. The sloped pasture between him and the safety of the barn was not only covered with water, but rapidly becoming a sea of mud sliding toward the gully. Toward him.

One frantic glance in each direction confirmed the barn was his only hope, so he gulped in a breath and fought for every foothold while rain pummeled his already drenched hide.

With his tail dragging in the mud, he focused on the barn, and doggedly continued, half swimming, half climbing up what had begun as a slope but now felt like a mountain.

Ears flat, he slogged on. And on. And on. Until the terrain leveled off, assuring him he was closer. But the mud was different here, deep and thick, and there were hills and ditches where the horses and the tractor had dug through half-frozen snow.

Stanley staggered and nearly fell into a deep rut, caught himself at the last second and with all four legs spread out, braced, he stood gasping for breath. Didn't think he could move another step. He was done.

That's when he looked toward the barn and, through the driving rain, could make out what looked like dozens of cats standing just inside the door. *Good grief, I can't die here, covered in muck, with everyone watching.*

You're nearly there. He knew that voice. Tony, the guardian cat had visited him now and again when he first settled in at the ranch. *You can do this, Stanley.*

I don't think so.

A large tabby with a bent ear materialized in front of him. *I'll walk the last few steps with you.*

Swaying where he stood, on legs so terribly heavy just the thought of moving exhausted him, he knew he was finished. In less than a year he'd outwitted coyotes and dogs, outrun a marauding tractor, survived being trampled by a horse, lived through more blizzards than he could count, and here he was, about to lose his last life to a lousy rain storm. *Death by mud.*

Not on my watch.

Stanley's feet had sunk so deep, his belly touched the mud. He could just give up now, lie there and die. But he wasn't a quitter.

One at a time, he dragged his feet out. Braced again. Tilted sideways and barely caught himself.

Help's coming.

Two big tabbies bounded from the barn and flanked him, propped him up while he gritted his teeth and moved one foot, another. It didn't take nearly as much effort to move now they were almost lifting him off his feet.

The barn was getting closer, and the cats in the doorway began to cheer him on.

Come on, Stanley, you can do it.

Come on, Stanley!
You've got this!
Push, Stanley.
You're almost here!

Dozens of voices chiming in somehow made it easier to follow the guardian leading the way to the barn, one step at a time.

When he faltered, the encouragement got louder and louder, gave him enough courage and energy to make the journey.

When he collapsed just inside the door Tony touched him, nose to nose. Then his image faded, but Stanley could still feel the guardian's presence while a dozen or more cats worked on his drenched coat and muddy legs until he had recovered enough to sit up.

If you can climb, you should go to the loft, said one of the tabbies who'd helped him finish his journey. *It's much safer up there.*

Others were quick to chime in.

Not that there are any predators out in this weather.

There's food.

And water up there.

And soft places to rest.

Voices blended together, and he could do nothing but stare.

Cats he barely knew—and some he'd never laid eyes on before today—were there for him, helping him through a terrible ordeal.

Why? You don't even know me. Why have you done this?

You're one of us.

But I've been living over there in the supply yard, away from everyone. I've not been friendly at all.

Doesn't matter. You're still family.

Thank you.

Tony materialized in the middle of the group. *Welcome home, Stanley.*

And his image faded.

3

GYPSY

Gypsy stared at the empty dishes. Usually at this time of day, one was filled with kibble, and the other with fresh water, but there was no one here to put fresh food or water in them. Even the giant water bowl in the bathroom was empty, and there were no drips coming from any of the taps. Desperation was setting in.

You'll be too weak if you wait any longer. The guardian cat's voice slipped into Gypsy's mind again. *You made good progress yesterday.*

But not good enough. She still couldn't fit through the window, even though she spent hours trying to widen the opening. She needed to get it done, because tomorrow she'd be weaker still.

Today you'll get it open far enough.

Was the guardian certain? Or just saying what he knew Gypsy needed to hear? Didn't matter, she needed to get to work.

Until recently, she ran when she went up the

stairs to the bedroom, but now she was reduced to climbing slowly, bones and muscles aching from hours spent hard at work the day before.

The faint whiff of fresh air was encouraging, a great reminder of what she was fighting for. What waited just beyond her reach.

With a tiny spurt of energy, she hopped up and balanced on the wide ledge while trying for about the hundredth time to stuff her head through the narrowly open window...and, for the hundredth time, no matter how she shoved and twisted, she couldn't get through.

Resigned to the work, and uplifted by the progress so far, she shifted way off to one side, dug in with her back feet to brace, then started clawing and dragging at wooden frame. When she felt the tiniest movement, excitement fueled a frenzy of scraping, and tugging, and clawing until she lost her balance and landed on the carpet below.

On and on she fought for freedom, with the gains seeming insignificant until, after what felt like forever, when she was on the floor for the thousandth time, recouping her energy, she glanced up and anticipation rippled through her. In a single leap, she was at the opening, holding her breath, tipping her head sideways—and she was through! With her head free of the prison, she writhed, wriggled and thrashed until her shoulders were popped through, then...

Oh. Well. Good gravy. She hadn't thought about this part.

Balanced on the window's ledge, half in and half out, she was mortified to find herself somewhat suspended in midair, with nothing between her and the ground—which was a very long way down.

Now would be a good time for help from her guardian. *Tony?*

You have the tools. Now you need to find a safe place to land.

Gypsy surveyed her surroundings searching for something resembling a landing she could aim for...and found nothing. However, the logs were very weathered. If she could sink her nails into them and get to the corner of the building, the ends of the logs could be negotiated like steps.

Twisting so she could reach up beside the opening and get a good grip, she squeezed her ribs out, then hopped to get her hips to come through one at a time.

Clinging to the logs, she worked her way toward the corner. Then, without daring to rest for even a second, she painstakingly moved one foot at time, inching downward.

She made it about halfway before hugging the ends of the logs had her muscles screaming and her aching toes on fire. She gave up. Jumped. Landed in the tall grass with a soft thud.

Gypsy hunched there for a moment, motionless, while she waited for her heart to slow down. She was out. She was safe.

Well, not exactly. Now she was a target for predators, her bright calico coat like a beacon in the pale, dried grass. Slinking close to the ground, she circled the house, scooting from one bit of cover to the next, until she reached the place where she'd watched other animals drink while she was sitting in the window, wishing she was allowed to go outside.

The water was clear and cool, and seemed to be bubbling up from the ground. Gypsy drank and drank and drank until her belly was sure to be dragging, but she felt much better for it.

Now she needed food. She'd occasionally hunted mice in the house. Perhaps she could find one outdoors, too. She scooted to the woodshed as soon as she remembered her person had said the indoor mice came from the woodpile.

Gypsy found herself a spot up high enough to be out of reach if a coyote happened by, but low enough to pounce on any tiny critter that showed itself. Her tummy growled and made her impatient.

Tony?

Yes, Gypsy.

Thank you for helping me get out of the house, I'd surely have died there.

True, but you have several lives left.

Hmm. She'd think about that comment later. *If my person isn't coming back anytime soon, perhaps I should find somewhere else to live. The cats that come by here from time to time speak of a barn, and endless food. Could you help me find my way to such a place?*

You can find your own way, Gypsy. Just like depending on your claws to escape the house, you have the tools, senses that will lead you to the place the others spoke of.

Great, another puzzle. But he *did* say she could get there. Senses meant tasting, or seeing, or smelling, or touching.

When she used to sit in the window and watch

the goings-on outdoors, she often spotted cats working their way up the hill, through the trees. She did a careful visual scan, looking for a path to follow, but she was too far away.

She didn't think taste would be any help to her, unless imagining the taste of food would lead her in the right direction. Perhaps when she got closer.

Touch? Would she feel the path they took? Would the ground be worn smooth from many softly padded feet?

And smell. She often saw coyotes crossing the field, nose in the air, as though following the scent of their prey into the trees. Could she, too, follow the scent? But wouldn't it make her the prey as well?

Trees. As long as she kept her wits about her, she could dodge predators by climbing trees.

With a thin plan in her mind, she stayed close to the outbuildings for as far as they went toward the forest, then sprinted across the open field to get to the safety of the trees. She discovered there were many obstacles like bushes and logs and things to navigate, and she not only picked up the scent of other cats, but quickly spotted places where they had scratched on saplings and branches that lay on the ground.

She was on the right track, and even found a few paths she could follow. Until another scent filled her nostrils and she froze. Hair stood up on her back and her tail puffed out when a deer stepped out from between two trees. They stared at each other for a moment. Then the deer moved on, and Gypsy let out a long breath.

Freezing on the spot wasn't exactly a healthy reaction, was it? Shouldn't she have scooted up a tree to safety? What if...

Beating herself up was counterproductive, and wasn't getting her any closer to a meal. Pushing the event...well, non-event really...to the back of her mind, she again concentrated on following the scents of the other cats, and soon found the trees thinning, and buildings coming into sight at the bottom of a grassy hill.

She'd have to move out into the open again, and for some reason was very nervous this time. Gypsy climbed up onto an old stump and studied the area—looking for trouble, or a way to avoid putting herself at risk.

If she went way to the left, she'd be farther from her goal, but there was a fence she could follow, or climb up on and stay safely above the ground. Of course that would make her a sitting duck for a hawk, wouldn't it? But could a bird actually pick her up and carry her away? She wasn't exactly tiny, but she didn't weigh much right now, not after all those days without eating.

Maybe it would be best to scoot and scurry, but stay on the ground, using the fence as protection from above.

Frustrated because there was no easy answer, she considered calling on Tony, but thought better of it. He'd told her she could get to the food using the tools she had. Not much chance he'd tell her what to do now that she had the barn in sight. It looked just like the other cats had described. A huge thing built of logs, with a wide-open top area where hay was stored. She could actually see the hay from here, and that's where the safe haven and food were.

Use my tools.

Gypsy did a careful visual scan. Listened for the slightest sound, and tested the air for scent. Nothing, nothing, and nothing. She took a deep breath, jumped down and, as fast as her legs could carry her, sprinted alongside the fence until she reached a place with a path obviously worn by many cats.

She didn't slow down, didn't worry about predators, just let her instincts guide her along a well-traveled path, up onto some barrels, across the roof of a shed, down to the fence rails surrounding a horse pen, and up the tall post to the loft.

She made it.

Standing at the edge of the loft, she caught her breath and took in her new surroundings. Buckets and boxes were stacked for as far as she could see, but again, there were worn paths to follow, and soon she was able to see the giant stack of hay, and right there in front of her, the big blue barrel she'd heard about, and it truly did have holes in the bottom where kibble was falling out. Her mouth watered and hunger ripped at her insides.

She glanced around. *Hello?*

A large tabby poked his head out from between a few bales stacked off to one side.

Hi.

I'm Gypsy, and my person, the one from the log house way up the hill, hasn't come home in a long time, and I have no food, so I've come here hoping

33

to get something to eat.

Help yourself. Everyone's welcome here.

Thank you.

She needed no further urging. Dove in. Scooped up huge mouthfuls, and swallowed without bothering to chew.

When she couldn't fit another morsel into her belly, she finally came up for air, and that's when the prickling of her skin registered. She glanced over her shoulder and was disconcerted to see dozens of cats staring at her from every nook and cranny. She turned slowly, then edged backwards. Bumped into something soft and hopped away. *Oh!*

Hi, I'm called Peep. The tiny ginger wore a welcoming expression. *Who are you? Where did you come from?*

I'm Gypsy. I lived in a cabin over the hill, but my person has gone away to a place called prison and won't be coming back. Should she mention she only knew this because the guardian told her?

Welcome to the barn, Gypsy. Everyone here is pretty chill. No one will bother you unless you do something dangerous. Then they'll let you know.

I can't imagine doing something dangerous. She just wasn't that kind of cat. Sure, she'd just escaped through a second story window and run nearly two miles, but she'd have starved to death otherwise. And now her belly was full, all she wanted was a nice long nap. And as soon as she said as much to her new friend, she was led to the haystack.

There are lots of places tucked way inside here, but most of them are occupied. Probably better if

34

you choose somewhere on the outside. There's kind of a nook over here. Come on, I'll show you.

It was a good spot, where Gypsy could put her back against a bale and safely drop off to sleep.

Peep settled in beside her. *I'll hang with you for a while if you don't mind. I always find it safer to sleep when someone else is close by. Not that predators can get up here or anything, but still...*

The long days and nights of pacing inside the empty house, plus the hard work of getting the window open, and her journey, had taken a toll. Gypsy could barely keep her eyes open. *Thanks.*

When unfamiliar odors tickled her awake, she sat bolt upright, eyes wide. Hay. She was surrounded by hay. And there was Peep, the tiny ginger. Memories flooded back, and she forced her muscles—gone tense and ready to flee—to relax.

You had a long sleep. Do you feel better?

Thirsty. Very thirsty. And her belly hurt a bit.

Come, I'll take you to the water. Once on ground level, they circled around behind a giant metal cylinder standing on end at the side of the barn.

What is that?

It's called a silo. The people store grain inside, for feeding the horses. A truck comes and puts it in through the top, and the people use that small door at the bottom to get it out. Just like our kibble feeder, but the grain is very noisy when it goes in because there's a truck and a tractor running too. I hide in the machine shop until it's over.

Good to know. She'd have to find out where this safe shop was. But meantime, Peep had stopped

35

beside a large squarish thing, about three or four feet high. The ground around the far end of it was all wet, and quite muddy.

This is the trough. It's where we get water. The edge is rounded and not very wide, so take care when you jump up, or you'll get a dunking.

Gypsy hesitated.

It's not as scary as it sounds. You won't drown if you fall in, and it's easy to drink from. The water is from a spring, so the trough is always filled right to the edge. Well, at least at that end, because it's on a bit of a slope.

Peep sure knew a lot. And made everything sound less scary, sort of. And the other cats all managed there, didn't they?

Peep hopped up onto the rim. *Come on.*

Gypsy made the leap and was quite pleased with her balance as she walked the edge behind the tiny ginger. Peep stopped and turned so all four feet were side by side and pointed toward the water. Then crouched over and lapped it up.

It looked easy enough, but Gypsy's feet were as wide as the ledge, and it was rounded, which made balancing even more difficult.

Come on, Gypsy, you can do it.

Of course she could.

Gulp.

She concentrated. Slowly turned her body, but when she tried to move her left hind foot around to balance on the outside of her left front, she teetered badly. Was barely able to catch herself and regroup.

Took a breath, made the slow turn. And nearly cheered when she managed to get her feet aligned beside each other, just like the little ginger's. She could do this. She leaned down toward the water and her feet started to slip.

Oh no. She shuffled her weight back quickly, but then she was in danger of falling over backwards. Wobbling back and forth, nearly out of control, she fought for balance.

Get lower.

Lower would be a swim she didn't want... But wait. Peep had been crouching, not leaning.

Gypsy lowered quickly, dispersing her body weight more evenly, and the wobbling stopped.

There, you've got it. But watch—

A horse nose was suddenly right in her face, and she nearly toppled over backwards. Only moving her eyes, she glanced up. It wasn't a horse at all. It was Dickens, the old donkey she'd met only a few months ago when Jonah, Gypsy's owner, locked him in the mudroom for two days until his person came and paid money for him, and for the damages.

Have a heart, Dickens, don't make me fall in the water.

I thought you might want to lean on me while you drink. Just until you get the hang of it.

Oh, well, that would be good. Thanks.

Least I can do for an old friend.

Gypsy did lean against him, and took a long drink. She was pretty certain she could have done it without his help, but she liked the warm, soft fur on the side of his face, and his warm breath surrounding her. When she'd had her fill, she hopped back down to where Peep was waiting for her.

It was you who helped Dickens when he was kidnapped?

I didn't do all that much.

You kept me company when I was afraid. And there were the peaches.

Peep tipped her head sideways like a curious dog. *Peaches?*

I had no food or water, so Gypsy pushed jars of peaches off a shelf after the man went away in his truck. I didn't know peaches and peach juice were so delightful.

We were just lucky your person came for you the same time as Jonah came back. After you left, there was a lot of shouting about how he should have put a bullet in you instead of offering to let the man have you back.

Sounds like your person was a bad man.

Not always. He treated me okay most of the time. Talked to me a lot, anyways. About stuff he was going to do, places he'd go one day, ways he'd get even with people who owed him. He was angry a lot, except when he smoked at night. Then he got mellow, and opened toona for himself, but always shared a bit with Gypsy.

Dickens looked relieved. *He's not going to come here looking for you?*

Nope.

She'll be one of us now, a loft cat.

And if you miss your soft indoor living, you can sit on me sometimes.

Gypsy looked up at the donkey's fluffy back. She'd bet it was softer than the sofa she'd left behind, and warmer, too. Friends weren't something she ever had before, but she had a feeling becoming a loft cat was going to suit her just fine.

KATHRYN JANE

4

ALBERT & BRAZIL

Albert didn't care much for cats. Not that he
had anything against those of his own species. He
was simply a loner.

Instead of living in the barn with the rest of the
feline community, he made a home for himself
under one of one outbuildings. His size made it
difficult at first, but every day he dug and worked at
expanding his space, so now it was quite nice and
roomy once he navigated the narrow entrance. And
if he worked his way to the outer edges, he could
see through the cracks, and got a kick out of
watching the antics of the resident goats and
guardian llama.

But everything changed when a half-grown
silver tabby dove under the shed one day. Poor little
thing had been terrified.

Albert could have chased her out, sent her
scurrying to the barn, but knew what it was like to
land here without a clue what to do, where to go,

how to survive. He'd been mentored when he arrived, which made it his duty to take on this youngster, who said her name was Brazil. He'd help her acclimate once she got a good night's sleep.

First thing in the morning, Albert took her to the loft—a fancy name for the second floor of the barn, which was nothing more than a wide expanse of planks worn smooth and shiny by years and years of hay storage. A colony of feral cats lived among the sweet-smelling bales of hay stacked to the rafters at one end, and the jumble of junk like old barrels and buckets and wagons and things at the other. In the middle was a wide-open space where the feeding station was set up, not far from the square hole in the floor where the ladder came up from below.

Oddly, even though the lower level was made of giant logs piled on their sides, this upper deck had nothing but a few upright logs supporting the high tin roof. Albert, a cat who had lived indoors with humans for the first five years of his life, found the lack of walls extremely disconcerting.

Being a less than agile cat, he could potentially fall right off the edge while stalking prey...or worse, what if he was suddenly spooked by something and hopped sideways or backwards, simply from reflex? Landing on the hard ground below could mean a broken bone or two, or a lurking predator could grab him before he got his wits back.

According to Zak, his mentor, no such horrific event had ever occurred, but it didn't mean it couldn't happen. Albert was taking no chances. Having once experienced a life-changing fall—and learning not all cats landed on their feet—he stayed as far away from that precipice as possible

Albert?

He shot a glance at the striped cat making his way down from high up among the bales. *Hey, Zak.*

Where's the new kid?

Right behind me. Albert glanced over his shoulder, expecting the youngster to pop up through the opening, but nothing happened. *Well, she was here a second ago.*

Hopping down to the lower level, they found her balanced on a narrow beam.

Hello, Brazil.

Her pupils rounded, making her eyes suddenly more black than green. *How do you know my name?*

Your friend Albert told me.

Albert wasn't at his best when trying to balance, but managed to peek around his friend. *This is Zak. He's sort of an ambassador for the colony.*

It's true, Brazil. I'll introduce you to the others, and you need not be afraid anymore.

I'm not afraid. Her voice wobbled.

Then come along. It's time you met the others. You'll stay with me, Albert?

I promise. And Albert, unlike the people who had dumped him here after they grew bored with him, kept his promises.

When they showed Brazil the enormous blue barrel with holes in the bottom where an endless supply of kibble leaked out, she forgot her fears and dug right in, obviously famished.

A large tuxie, one nearly identical to Albert,

approached.

Dennison, this is Brazil.

The new cat kept a respectable distance from the ravenous youngster. *That's an odd name.*

My person said her dream was to someday live in Brazil.

If you have a person, why are you here?

A man came to live with us, and he sneezed a lot, so I wasn't allowed in the bedroom anymore, and then he said it was him or me.

You got dumped because your person got a boyfriend? This new voice came from behind Brazil. *That sucks.*

Then another chimed in. *Same thing happened to me.*

It's called allergies, added a third. *People sneeze a bunch, and then we have to fend for ourselves.*

Spooked by so many new voices, Brazil spun around, expecting to see dozens of cats right behind her, but there were just a few watching from high in the haystack.

Once her belly was filled, Albert continued her tour, taking Brazil to the tack room on the first level of the barn.

*It smells quite...*she hesitated...*odd, but in a comfortable way—if that makes any sense.*

It did. Albert loved it in here. *Horse sweat. The only thing better to roll on is horse poop.*

Really?

Yep.

Brazil would reserve judgement on that. She'd smelled poop from dogs, cats, and people, and found nothing appealing about any of it. But this sweet scent was intriguing, pulling her closer.

Where is it coming from?

Those thick woven blanket things over the saddles.

Saddles?

Hmm. They're what people sit on when they ride the horses.

Brazil popped up onto the long rail filled with saddles, and climbed over them, rubbing against the rough material of the blankets, then just lay there, as though not planning to move for a while.

This is a good place to hang out if you don't mind humans, but they could bring dogs with them, so sleeping on the saddles isn't a good idea—in the daytime at least.

She got the message, and they moved on to the feed room next. *This is the best spot for hunting. Mice and rats come in to steal grain. Chipmunks, too, sometimes.* Brazil's blank expression made him laugh.

You'll need to learn how to hunt, unless you're okay with living on kibble from the barrel.

And from the look on her face, she was, so Albert took her to another source, a building almost as tall as the barn. *This is the machine shop. Watch this.* He stood on his hind legs and pushed at the small square several feet from the ground until it swung inward.

A kitty door, she said, *like the one to get to my litter box in the laundry room.*

Great, you know how to use one. Come on, then. Albert jumped, and when his front feet pushed, the flap opened, and he sailed through the opening.

But when Brazil tried to follow, she hesitated after she pushed the door and it swung back, smacking her in the nose. *Ah-Chew!*

Albert winced. *You have to do it all in one move, jump like you're going through the hole, as though the door isn't even there. Your feet will hit and make it open at just the right second.*

I don't know if I can do that.

Of course you can. Come on.

Brazil sat back and thought about her approach. Steeled herself for another whack in the face, and made the leap.

Swoosh! And she was suddenly inside a cavernous place that smelled like the inside of the truck she'd been in when she got here. The floor was smooth and cold like ice, and there were shelves against all the walls, as well as a wide table Albert hopped up on.

They leave food here on the workbench sometimes, but the dishes aren't very big, and get empty fast.

Brazil joined him, and Albert pointed at a hole in the ceiling.

You can get up in the attic that way. Just have to climb the shelves.

What's up there?

Don't know, but the others tell me it's nice, and a good spot in the winter, because the people light a fire in the woodstove when they come in here, and it stays warm for a long time.

By the time they'd toured the rest of the

barnyard, Brazil was hungry again, so they went back to the loft. Once their bellies were full, instead of going back to Albert's home under the shed, they burrowed between bales down low on the stack and settled in for an afternoon snooze.

Albert woke to Brazil screaming his name. He bolted from their nest, eyes wide and ears swiveling. *Where are you?*

Down here!

Slinking on his belly, Albert reached the edge of the loft and peered over. Nothing. But then Zak called out, *She's on the silo. You'll have to climb over the stack.*

How could she be on the silo—a large round tower made of metal, with a pointed, cone-shaped roof? There was nothing to be *on*, so that didn't make a whit of sense.

Albert scrambled over the stack to where dozens of cats were perched on a wide expanse of floor at the edge of the loft. They were all staring across an expanse of about ten feet to where Brazil was clinging precariously to the top edge of the silo, where the smooth roof met the corrugated sides.

Albert couldn't quite believe his eyes. Mentor a youngster, they'd said. It's fun, they said. Huh. *Brazil?*

Help!

What—

I'm stuck.

How—

I—

Not important, said Zak.

You're right, of course. How are we going to

get her down?

Good question. The ground between the barn and silo was covered with concrete.

She'll bust a leg for sure if she jumps. She was level with the loft, so if she continued around the circle of the edge, couldn't she just jump back to the barn? He gauged the distance, and conceded it was farther than *he* could jump without a running start.

Look up.

Just two words from a voice Albert hadn't heard in a long time—not since the guardian warned him of imminent danger once before—and Albert spotted the circling hawk.

It was a long way off yet, but Albert remembered when his brothers were taken by an owl. The whole litter had been playing just outside the barn, and they thought the owl was too far away to be a threat.

Without looking down, without thinking about what he was about to do, Albert backed up as far as he could, then raced toward the edge of the loft and launched himself into the air.

He landed hard on the smooth metal of the cone, and fought the urge to try digging in with his claws, instead sliding, sliding, sliding slowly down toward Brazil—he hoped! Because he couldn't see where he was going, and needed to somehow manage to land beside her, not on top of her.

You're good, Albert, coached Zak. *Almost there.*

He flexed his toes, and when his hind feet hit the roll of the edge, he dug in. Held on. Twisted so his front end slid down, putting him directly behind the tiny silver tabby, making it impossible for the hawk to grab her.

Now, to try to breathe and not panic.

Brazil turned halfway around to face him. *What are you doing here?*

Good question. *I could ask the same.*

Well, there was this butterfly, and it was dancing in the sunbeam.

You leapt out here to catch a butterfly?

Um, no, not really. I was just playing, chasing it for fun, because it was so happy and made me laugh...and then suddenly I was tipping off the edge and couldn't scramble back, so I jumped over here instead.

I suppose it seemed like a good idea at the time.

Exactly. Better than falling, right?

Albert dared a glance over the edge, but when the earth below him began to swirl drunkenly, he averted his eyes and fought for focus. *Right.*

Are you going to help me get down?

Get down? Uh...well.

They had to get off of here somehow, and straight down was a bad choice. Very, very bad. Heck, he'd rather jump into a pool of water than hit that concrete—and water was right up there with heights on the list of things that terrified him.

But wait. Wasn't there a water trough around the back of this thing? And wouldn't that be a less disastrous place to land in spite of the...well, water? He squelched a full-body shudder.

Zak?

I'm here.

Have a look around the back. Could we make it

to the trough?

A general murmuring of speculation filled the air while Zak and the other cats made their way to a better vantage point.

Yep, you can do it, and it's full. Gives you a couple of feet less to fall, and all that water to slow you down at the end. I think it's your best choice.

Water? Brazil glanced over her shoulder at Albert. *Like a bath? No way.*

Albert understood her aversion, but didn't think she understood what a dire situation they were in. *Just follow the ledge around, and you'll see it.*

The slightly downward bend made keeping one's balance a bit of a chore, but they eventually made it to where they could see their best—make that only—option.

The huge plastic tub was about six feet long and two feet wide, so it shouldn't be too hard a target to hit, but being three feet deep meant an awful lot of water would close over his head and—

Cats of all shapes and sizes were gathering around the trough. Albert let out the breath he hadn't realized he was holding. They had his back. They'd be there if something went wrong, rescue Brazil if she needed help, because he'd still be up here.

Are you ready?

I'm not going first.

You have to.

Nuh-uh.

Look up. Albert waited, and when she suddenly flattened her body to the metal, he knew she'd seen the hawk circling above. *You're the perfect size for him to scoop up and take to his nest. But he won't bother with me because I'm too big. Once you jump, the other cats will be there to block him from getting to you.*

I'd rather land on that pillow than in the water. Pillow?

He followed her line of sight. Well, yes, the llama did look like a giant, soft pillow, since he hadn't been clipped in years.

What do you think, Elliott? She probably doesn't weigh more than about three pounds.

I've never been called a pillow before, but the goats jump all over me, so I'm sure I can handle a cat. He ambled over to stand beside the trough. *Is this close enough?*

Brazil peered over the side. *I s'pose.*

Albert peeked over too. *If you overshoot, at least you'll land in the water.* He didn't want to think about what would happen if she landed short of the target.

No, that wasn't going to happen. She'd be fine. He'd be fine. All would be well, and he could go back to his simple existence, where he was safely on the ground at all times.

But at nearly the same time as the thought of safety gelled, a butterfly danced just out of reach, and Brazil crouched as though she was going to spring.

Oh, for heaven's— *Brazil!*

Her body jerked and she swung to stare at him. *What?*

You need to focus on getting off of here before you think about playing.

51

She hung her head, then glanced at him out of the corner of her eye. *I just can't seem to help it. I go after them before I even know I'm going to.*

You'll be running out of lives if you don't get a handle on that. I'll work on it with you later. But for now, get a bead on your landing spot.

With a sigh she shifted and appeared to concentrate on the broad white back. *Ready.*

What about you, Elliott?

Ready.

Okay, incoming. Go for it, Brazil.

And she leapt. Sailed through the air to land with a soft thud in the middle of the llama's back. A small puff of dust rose from his thick coat, and dozens of voices cheered. Cats, goats, horses, and even cattle had gathered close.

Great. Albert had to jump now, and the only thing worse than being perched this far off the ground was voluntarily hurling himself into midair, hoping—of all things—to land in water deep enough to drown in.

Of course, staying put would not only be foolish, but make him look like a cowardly idiot— in front of every creature on the ranch.

Albert?

Oh, great. It was never a good sign when a guardian cat communicated. *Am I about to use up another life, Tony?*

That's your choice, my friend. The concrete below is deadly. But you do have a viable option.

You think I can make it.

I know what you're considering is not impossible, but I'm here to tell you that doubt will

52

land you short of your mark.

Well that wasn't what he wanted to hear. Albert swallowed hard. *It's not that I don't think I can make the distance, it's just...*

Just what?

I'm average. I'm not daring. I don't want to be the center of attention, but everyone is watching me. Expecting me to do this bold thing and...

And?

And knowing the water will close over my head when I land, and they'll all be watching when I come up coughing, and choking...

And alive.

And a spectacle. What if, when he was leaping off, that image got in the way and he screwed up, missed altogether? Then he'd be a dead spectacle, or worse, broken and alive, and everyone would stare while he dragged his shattered body to the barn.

Albert sighed, wishing he could wind back time to when he was enjoying his quiet, solitary morning snooze.

A murmuring arose from the crowd of onlookers—probably speculating whether or not he'd make the jump, or perhaps guessing why he hadn't done it yet.

Dickens the donkey let out a mighty bray and headed toward the silo, followed by about a dozen horses. They effectively covered the entire area between Albert and the water trough and beyond, while cats hopped up and balanced on the rim.

A giant lump formed in Albert's throat, and without another moment of hesitation, he focused on the target, launched himself into the air, and experienced every passing second as though it was a minute long.

The water glinted, surrounded by the blurred colors of horses and cats. The wind was an odd sensation whizzing past his widespread toes, and made a roaring sound in ears he'd laid flat.

Closer, closer it came. Circling his tail madly to maintain his balance and make sure he landed feet first, he held his breath, pinched his nostrils closed, and the water seemed to come up and grab him, pluck him from the air. Drag him down under.

The impact against his belly drove the air from his lungs while cool water enveloped him, poured into his ears, and went up his nose and down his throat.

Then his feet hit the bottom, and he pushed off, burst through the surface, front legs outstretched, reaching for the side, which he managed surprisingly quickly, because there was something pushing him from behind.

Albert dragged himself up, but again had help from behind, so when he was able to gain purchase on the edge, he glanced back and discovered the source of the help.

Dickens. With a silly grin and a dripping wet face.

Thanks.

Welcome. Dickens tipped his head, which made his long ears sort of flop around his head. *You good now?*

I think so.

We're gone, then. And he sauntered away, with

the small herd of horses trailing in his wake.

Albert dropped to the ground so he could have a good shake to get the rest of the water out of his ears, then started cleaning up—not much liking the bits of slimy green stuff stuck to his coat—and a tickling began inside his nose.

Achew!

Bless you, said Brazil from her perch on the llama.

What does that mean?

I don't know, but it's what the lady I lived with said whenever her boyfriend sneezed.

Oh. Albert searched the sky for the predator, then shot her another glance. Probably safe enough with the llama for protection, but still.

Why are you still up there?

Elliott is my friend now, and said he doesn't mind if I hang out with him.

The llama turned his head so he could see the small cat. *I'm not staying here any longer, though, so unless you want to go with me, you should probably get off now.*

Where are you going?

To the short grass by the house, for a snooze.

Oh, well. The llama moved just when she started to jump, and what happened next would remain the highlight of the day. Brazil's jump to the ground became an unintended leap into the water trough.

She came to the surface sputtering, with Elliott using his nose to push her toward the side, where she climbed up and out, landing next to Albert and shaking water from her ears.

She sneezed.

Bless you, said Elliott. And there was a resounding chorus of 'bless yous' that made Brazil giggle...and right then she knew this was where she belonged.

5

THOMAS

Cold. So, so cold. The winter storm hit hard, and wasn't leaving anytime soon. Thomas curled into an even tighter ball, but the wind cut a path through his fur.

This wasn't going to work. He'd surely freeze to death tonight.

The others had invited him to their spot deep within the bales stacked on the far corner of the loft, but he'd never liked it in there. Went in a few times when he first arrived at the ranch, but it was hot back then, and the air in the hiding place very stuffy…just like the other cats.

He sure could use some of that hot air now, but the wind would surely blow him off the rafters if he tried to climb up into the loft, especially since the cold was making his legs so stiff and hard to move.

He needed shelter. Had tucked in between the wall and a short stack of straw bales, but the wind was getting in here, and the bales weren't tightly interwoven like the hay, and provided less protection from the bitter wind.

Thomas crept along the narrow space until he found a spot where he could wiggle between bales, and then he lucked out. There was a slot where he could drop down and get underneath.

He wriggled and twisted, shoved and dug, until he was firmly wedged right in the middle of the small stack. Not as deep a nest as the cats up in the loft, but the best protection he could get without trying to traverse the deadly rafters and ledge when he was too stiff and cold to climb safely.

Wishing he'd thought to fill his belly before the storm started, he drifted off to sleep with visions of bowls filled with kibble, like he had in the barn where he was born.

Oh, how cozy it had been in the pile of sweet-smelling horse blankets tucked into a corner of the tack room. Back then he had his mamma and siblings to snuggle with, and a nice man to play with when he came to feed them.

The man made toys for them from bale twine and crumpled paper, and brought food Mama loved, and the kittens got to like it after a while, too. At first Thomas didn't understand how to eat it, but he eventually caught on, and looked forward to when the man visited each day and opened a new can for them.

Just when they got big enough to really have fun and try escaping from the safety of the barn, a stranger came and put Thomas and his brother Martin in a cage and carried them out to a truck. They huddled together, terrified for many hours, and when the truck stopped and the cage was opened, they ran as fast as they could to the nearest dark place and hid there until nighttime. That's when they crept out and discovered they were in another horse barn, with straw-filled stalls and a loft up above.

An enormous tabby cat showed them where the food was, and several other cats greeted them, but once a few days passed and the boys were no longer afraid, they discovered how much fun it was to be free. Even though the others constantly warned them about taking dangerous risks, they climbed trees and ran down fence rails so fast they frightened the horses. Played on the giant, round bales of hay, hot-footed after squirrels, and teased the goats.

When winter came, they chased snowflakes and ran around like idiots in the snow, because it was a lot more fun than spending their days and nights huddled in the safety of the darn loft. The brothers loved life, and knew they were absolutely invincible.

Right up until Martin was grabbed by a coyote.

Thomas hadn't left the barn since. Stayed safe behind closed doors like his mama taught them only a few months earlier.

And he steered clear of the other cats. The ones who had repeatedly warned them of the dangers. Thomas couldn't bear to face them now. He lived mostly on the top edges of the stall walls, and only went to eat when he was certain no one else was around.

The only cat he ever talked to was Zak, the

huge brown tabby who was friends with everyone. Zak tried to get him to sleep upstairs in the hay, with the other cats, but Thomas still kept his distance. How could he accept the friendship of those he and Martin had laughed at for their stuffy ways? No, he'd stay in the lower half of the barn, where the goats and llama made camp at night.

One night, when the wind was blowing snow through the gaps in the log walls, and it was so cold it hurt to breathe, the goats and llama huddled so close together they looked like one giant creature.

Elliott's head came up from the pile. *Come and join us, Thomas. It will be warmer for you.*

Snuggle with the goats he and Martin had teased and laughed at because they chewed all the time and they smelled funny?

Thanks, but I've got a good spot here.

Thomas needed to look out for himself. To prove he was grown up now, and not a silly kitten any longer.

But he was having trouble staying warm tonight. Woke up once shivering so hard he'd bitten his tongue, and the taste of his own blood scared him for a minute or two. He glanced around as best he could—considering the air burned his eyes and he could barely move his head in such tight quarters—and saw nothing but crisp yellow straw.

A giant shiver wracked his body. Maybe he should go and join the others. What did it matter if they laughed at him, scolded him. He was going to freeze to death if he stayed here, so what difference did it make?

But an odd numbness slipped over him, and it

was almost warm, like sunshine, and the shivering stopped. And he got sleepy...very, very, sleepy...and a little voice in his head told him he should stay awake, but he just couldn't...and as he drifted off, the smooth warmth filled him, and he sighed.

Tired, oh so tired. And he drifted off to sleep.

Thomas! You need *to wake up now. The lady is here to help you.*

The strangely disembodied voice dragged him back to a place of semi-consciousness, but he couldn't get all the way awake.

She can't find you there. You need to come out so she can help you.

He tried again to move, but couldn't.

"Thomas!" The lady sounded frantic, and then her voice faded as he drifted off to where the sun was warm on his back and he could hear birds singing in the trees.

Are you coming across? Now *there* was a voice he recognized, and before long his brother Martin came into view, strolling across a colorful bridge. Thomas had a funny feeling in his heart. Had to sit down for a minute. And another voice slipped inside his head.

You don't have to go yet if you're not ready. Glancing over his shoulder, Thomas recognized the tabby with the crinkled ear. The one who was there when the coyote grabbed Martin. He said the same thing that day, about not going.

The lady is here to help if you decide to stay.

Thomas understood now. This was the rainbow bridge he'd heard stories about, where cats went when they ran out of lives.

It isn't your time yet.

But wouldn't it be wonderful to play with his brother again, and feel warm like this always?

He edged forward, and when Martin reached the place where the cobblestones ended, Thomas couldn't resist creeping closer and leaning over to touch foreheads in a move so familiar, more wonderful warmth spread through him. There was something different about Martin. He didn't seem cocky anymore. Instead, he was relaxed and happy.

"Thomas!" Oh dear, the lady again.

Now, Thomas. You must decide right now, said the guardian.

It's not your time yet, bro. Go with the lady for a while. I'll still be here to meet you when you come back. We'll all be here to welcome you to the other side.

Thomas sighed, and with a final head-butt, he backed away from the edge of the bridge.

Bright light and burning cold instantly assailed him, and he could hear the lady crying. She dragged away the rest of the bales and gently lifted him, then stuffed him inside her clothes where it was very warm, and everything went dark again. Muffled sounds were a blend of her calling Zak, and an engine and slamming doors.

Thomas didn't wake up again until the lady unzipped her coats and peeked at him. "Poor little thing, I think your eyes are frozen open."

He was lifted to another place then, again surrounded by warmth, like when he'd been surrounded by his littermates and snuggled in close to his mama. Thomas curled deeper into the heat and sleep took him away.

Occasionally a sound would rouse him, but not enough to make him open his eyes or move so much as a whisker, and he stayed that way for hours and hours and hours.

Until the wonderful smell of toona made his nose twitch and his tummy rumble.

Thomas stretched out first one front leg, then the other, spreading his toes wide until they bumped something hard and his eyes popped open.

There, right in front of him was a bowl with tiny pieces of toona in it. Well, that was surely reason enough to get him moving.

But he was wobbly when he tried to get to his feet, as though there was a great weight on his back.

A hand came into view, and lifted what had been weighing him down. Some sort of a blanket.

"There, that should help a bit." Then the lady pushed the dish right under his chin.

He leaned forward for a bite of the delectable food and discovered it was floating in a bunch of warm and tasty juice, which he eagerly lapped up, and by the time he stood to lick the far side he was feeling stronger. And his tummy felt better, but it was a long way from full.

Wide awake now, he skulked around the small room, sniffing and poking about, found a couple of good spots for hiding, and found a box filled with sawdust like the pile by the barn.

"That's your litter box," said the lady, and he nearly jumped because he'd forgotten she was there. "Where you can pee and poop."

No way. He'd just go outside. He hopped up to

the ledge of the big square opening to the outdoors and his nose smacked against something invisible. What the heck? He pawed at the clear thing covering the exit, and eventually decided there was no way out. Perhaps he *would* have to poop in that box.

Thomas was suddenly very tired again, and when he returned to the warm place where he'd been sleeping he realized it was actually a crate—like the one he'd been in for the ride to the ranch, but this one was huge. There was a blanket over the outside, and a white cord sticking out from the bottom.

The toona dish was still empty, but he could smell something else now, and pushed past the blanket he'd been wrapped in so he could investigate.

Careful, Thomas.

Startled, he hopped backwards.

Zak?

The tabby face suddenly appeared from amidst what Thomas had thought was a jumble of blankets in the crate.

Come back under here, you're starting to shiver again.

He hadn't noticed, but could feel the chill now, and burrowed in beside Zak, grateful for the warmth of his friend, and whatever was so toasty under them. When the lady removed the empty dish, his conscience niggled.

I'm sorry I ate all the toona, Zak. I didn't know you were here. I thought I was alone, and I was very hungry.

No worries. I've been eating all the while you were asleep. The toona was for you, because the lady said she hoped the smell would make you wake up.

Was I asleep for a very long time?

You were frozen solid. She thought you were dead at first, but she brought you here to try and thaw you. Brought me along to keep you company.

I met your friend Tony.

Means you have one less life now.

Somewhere deep inside he knew it was true. *He woke me up and told me to move so the lady could find me, but I didn't see him until I was at the bridge, and he said I could go with my brother but didn't have to. He had that funny ear, like you said, and was sort of grumpy-looking, but his voice was kind.*

That would be Tony, all gruff and nothing but a softy inside. He was nice to everyone, even the horrible little dogs who wanted to chase us. He said it wasn't their fault they were bred to chase. He made them crazy, though, because he'd just sit and stare them down.

What happened to him? How did he run out of lives?

Old age. He was twenty and his heart simply stopped one day.

Yet he stayed on as guardian.

I think he kind of owned the place. Had lived there through three different owners. He made it his duty to help new animals and people feel welcome, and I think he feared idleness on the other side. That's why he stayed to help out. He can cross back and forth at will, but stays on the other side more and more these days.

What about you? Will you cross when your time comes?

I don't know. Won't know until the choices are given to me.

Thomas understood, because he'd just been there and surprised himself. Why had he decided to stay somewhere he didn't feel comfortable, where he'd made a fool of himself and alienated the other cats? He didn't know the answer. At least not yet.

For two full days, he and Zak were kept in the small room. The lady stayed with them most of the time, talking lots, but staying quiet sometimes too, and at night she slept on the square thing she called a bed.

She told them about the changes she made so no one would ever freeze to death on her watch. "If I lived at the ranch, I'd just let everyone come inside, but since there's no way I can get the roof fixed on the house until summer, I've changed the woodstove in the machine shop to pellets, so I can leave the hopper stocked, and it will burn twenty-four/seven. I've also built a ramp from the workbench up to the attic, to make it easier to get up where it will be the warmest."

The warm part had Thomas's attention.

"What do you think? Are you two ready to go back? Or do you want to stay here with me?"

Stay here, like always? Thomas didn't like that idea.

Well, I guess until she has the house ready. How do I tell her no? I want to be outside.

You go over and scratch the door.
Really??
Yep. I was a housecat for ten years before I got dumped at the ranch.
Does that mean you'd rather stay indoors?
Oddly enough, no. I've grown used to my life now, and I have many friends in the loft.

There was an unpleasant reminder. Thomas didn't have any friends. He was alone but for Zak. Maybe he should stay here with the lady. She liked him, and didn't seem to mind that he'd been an idiot for a while.

Are you going to scratch the door, Zak?
Yes.

Thomas followed him, and copied his move, lifting a paw and touching the door, then letting the foot slide down. And the lady laughed.

"Well that's clear enough. I thought maybe you'd want to hang here with me, but I understand. It's a small space. I'd love to give you the run of the house, but I only pay for this one room, and the use of the kitchen, so I can't let you roam." She pulled on all the layers of clothing she wore to go outside.

"Once the rest of my inheritance comes in, I'll have the time and money to fix up the house, and we'll have a wonderful space where everyone can come and go as they please."

She held the crate door open. "You ready?"

Zak walked in, and Thomas followed. He would miss the daily toona treats, and that thing she called a heating pad, but he needed to stretch his legs again.

When they got to the ranch, she carried the

crate into the machine shop and closed the door. "See how warm it is in here with the new stove?"

She set the carrier on the workbench, then popped the top off a can of toona and set bits of it on a board angling up from where they were to a hole in the ceiling. "There you go, check it out," she said, and released them.

Thomas was quick to pop out and scarf down some of the delectable food, and was halfway up the ramp when he realized Zak wasn't with him.

Zak? There's toona.

But Zak was hunkered down getting major ear rubs, and apparently didn't care about toona. Thomas could eat it all if he liked. But that wouldn't be right. Instead, he only ate two more bits, then went up to investigate the attic.

It wasn't a huge space, but it *was* lovely and warm, and there were many old horse blankets to sleep on.

He went back down. *It's nice and cozy up there. I'll never have to freeze again.*

You'd not have frozen the first time if you'd joined the others in the haystack.

Zak was probably right. But still, Thomas wouldn't have to go there now, because he had this place.

He lay down beside Zak so he could get some petting too. He liked the lady's gentle hands a lot, especially when she scratched under his chin. It made his eyes close and the rumbling in his chest grow louder.

"I'm going to miss you two, but I understand why you want to be here. Since I found my own freedom, I know how amazing it feels." Zak leaned up against her and she smiled. "Once I can finally live here, my door will always be open, so if you ever have an urge to snuggle, you can stop by." She leaned down, snuggling Zak, and Thomas reared up to give her a head-butt, and she laughed.

"Maybe the whole colony will move in with me, and then I can really be a crazy cat lady."

She picked up the crate, then stroked them each one more time, from nose to tail. "Be good, boys." A gust of cold wind blew in when she left, and the kitty flap rattled when the door slammed.

Zak and Thomas sat there for a minute.

Will you move in with her, Zak?

A home, with a nice lady to love on me, and still be able to come and go and look after my friends? Yep, perfect life.

Thomas wondered if it was. He'd certainly liked being with the lady, but hated being indoors, except when she was there. If only the outdoors hadn't turned out to be so frightening.

I'm heading over to the barn. Zak stopped at the kitty door. *You coming, or staying here in the warm?*

There was food and water here, so he actually didn't need to leave, did he? But staying here would be no different than being locked indoors. Thomas hopped down off the workbench. *Wait for me.*

Following Zak, he walked the top fence rail and climbed up into the loft, expecting it to be quiet since everyone slept in the middle of the day. But instead, cats came from every nook and cranny, rushing toward them, and Thomas stood back so they could welcome their leader—then the most amazing thing happened.

They started crowding around Thomas, rubbing on him, butting heads, and their greetings washed over him.

We were worried.

Scared for you.

So happy.

Welcome home.

Stay in the hay with us.

Bro.

Thomas was overwhelmed by the trilling voices, head-butts, and full-body rubs, and there was a strange feeling growing deep inside him that made his whole body vibrate. A feeling half scary, half good.

He shot a glance at Zak. *I don't understand. Why are they being nice to me when I was never nice to them? Was rude and ignored them when they wanted to help me?*

It's called forgiving. It's what family does.

A place deep inside his chest where the cold had settled when he was taken from his mamma, a place the heating pad hadn't been able to reach, became warm again.

6

DAISY

You're almost there.

As it had for the past several weeks, the voice encouraged her to keep going. Daisy had yet to actually see Tony the guardian cat, but she listened when he promised to lead her to what he called a cat haven, where there was an endless supply of food and water, plus a safe nesting area where her next litter could be born.

She'd given birth to twenty-one litters so far, ninety-three kittens in all, and twenty-six survived past their first birthday in spite of illness, worms in their bellies stealing the food they ate, tomcats, predators, and cars. One of her daughters died giving birth less than a year after she was born, but several others went on to produce many kittens of their own.

Daisy was never one to dwell on those she lost, because there was always a new litter either in her belly or at her side, and they were the ones who needed all her time and energy. The past couldn't be changed, but the future was full of possibilities. That's why she left the farm where the bad dog lived. True, she was safe there as long as she stayed in the loft, and the man did provide food. But the space was small, and raising kittens where they had nowhere to roam and learn to hunt didn't seem like a good idea.

It was better to die trying to find somewhere they would have a hopeful future, and people she could trust to help her.

She'd had a good run of kind people throughout her life, but the one or two bad ones were hard to forget. Like the man who took her and her littermates away from their mama and gave them away in a parking lot.

After they'd all been taken but her, a lady came along on her bicycle, and the man told her he would have to drown the last kitten because it was black, and had a broken tail, so nobody wanted it.

Daisy—that's the name the lady gave her—was quickly scooped up and stuffed under a pink T-shirt for the ride home, where she was snuggled and played with in secret for almost a whole day before the husband person caught on.

He didn't want a black cat in his house.

Daisy was allowed to stay in the garage for a while, until one night he took her in the car and dumped her on the side of the road near a farm that became her home for the next four summers.

The people there were very nice, and always made sure there was food out for the dozens of strays who ended up there. It was quite wonderful when the lady had time to pet Daisy and talk to her, especially when she had a belly full of kittens, and was uncomfortable with all the kicking. That gentle, stroking hand seemed to calm the little ones too.

But then one day when a load of hay arrived for the cattle, Daisy did a silly thing. Unable to resist a wonderful smell, she followed her nose and climbed through the truck's open window to get to the tasty snack with a delectable middle, and she ate all three. Then, when she was licking the bottom of the container, it fell on the floor and she jumped down after it. That's when things went south.

The door opened, and a stranger was there, blocking her only avenue of escape, so she dove under the seat and stayed very still when what she should have done was raced out past him

When the window rolled up, she knew she was well and truly trapped. What to do?

The engine roared to life, and she must have been mesmerized by the vibration—or that's what she thought later, at least—because she didn't move for hours and hours.

When she did eventually peek out, the driver saw her and laughed.

"Where the devil did you come from?"

He shook his head. "Silly question. I wonder…" He said some numbers out loud, then Daisy heard the lady from the farm say hello, and the man said, "I think I've got a stowaway from your place. Black cat with huge green eyes."

"Oh, well, is there a pregnant belly attached and a tail with two bends in it?"

The man glanced at Daisy. "Can't see the tail,

but she's definitely round."

"She'd be one of the strays who showed up a few years ago. Very sweet, and not wild at all. If you don't want her, you can drop her back here anytime."

"We can always use another mouser. I'll look out for her."

He glanced at Daisy again. "I'm kinda glad you're here," he said. "I was thinking I'd lost my mind and forgotten I already ate the rest of the popcorn shrimp."

The man talked to her a lot then, and when the truck stopped, he let her out where there was a big barn with cows in it, and Daisy found a nice spot in the hay to have her kittens. In fact, she raised many kittens there over two summers before the wild-eyed dog came around and wiped out most of the cats, even got some of the toms coming to visit her.

That's when she knew it was time to leave.

She watched. And waited. Studied the habits of the creature who chased anything that moved, and the day he went galloping over the hill after a herd of elk, Daisy made a run for it in the opposite direction. Put miles between her and the place she called home. Didn't let herself think about the nice man who filled the food dishes in the loft every morning. She simply had to get away.

She followed a dry creek bed because the surrounding pines and fallen willows made good cover. And she could climb to safety if she spotted a predator, canine or otherwise. She travelled for days, covering miles and miles, certain she would eventually run into a farm or a house at least.

Instead there was nothing but wilderness, and survival became harder and harder. Squirrels were too darned tough to catch, and going after field mice meant risking her hide out in the open. Hunting in the daytime was safer since coyotes were out in full force at night, but Daisy's black coat made her stand out, and it meant she had to keep a careful watch on the sky for hawks. She was naturally careful, but extreme hunger changed that.

She was just about to go across an open field in search of mice when she first heard the voice. *You'll run out of lives very quickly if you do that.*

I'm starving to death anyway. What difference would it make? Was she talking to herself now? Just figuring out her next move? No, she'd definitely heard a strange voice.

My name is Tony, and I'm a guardian cat.

I've never heard of such a thing.

I used up my ninth life some time ago, but instead of crossing the rainbow bridge, I was given an opportunity to stay on this side and help out where I can.

What do you do exactly?

This and that. Mostly I coach when I come across a cat needing a helping hand. Since I don't have a physical presence, I'm only able to make suggestions, present arguments, and be an emotional shoulder to lean on.

Can you help me find food?

Absolutely. I'll guide you to a special place where there is always food for cats. It's a haven of sorts, and you'll like it there.

Funny how she trusted Tony right from the

start, even when she probably should have been suspicious, because he could have been a predator playing games with her mind.

But he wasn't, and he stayed with her for the rest of the journey. Guided her. Cheered her on.

At his urging, she trekked over a large hill—more like a small mountain—where bunch grass was so thick she had to wind her way through. But at least it provided a measure of cover. Other areas had short bushes to hide beneath or behind when she needed to slink past danger.

Weeks after leaving home, she was walking in the thin shade of a wooden fence when the barn came into view. Exactly as Tony had described, it was a massive log structure, with a wide-open loft stacked with hay on one end and mysterious shapes at the other. There was a silver grain silo and other, smaller, buildings as well.

She stopped for a moment and blinked to be certain she wasn't imagining the view.

It was real. She'd actually made it to the safe haven, and just in the nick of time. The litter currently dragging on her insides had been growing for weeks while she made her way here, taking everything she had in reserve when she couldn't find the food she needed. She'd been plump when she left, and was now little more than a skeleton with a big belly full of kittens ready to be born, soon. Very soon.

Desperately thirsty—since she hadn't been able to find a spring to drink from for days—when she spotted the huge water trough Tony told her about, she became a cat on a mission. Completely focused on her goal.

She nearly jumped out of her skin when something large and white suddenly materialized halfway between her and the barn.

It was a large, strange-looking creature. A rather ungainly thing, with a long neck and legs sticking out from a grimy mass of matted hair with bits of twigs and hay sticking out of it.

Having faith the voice would never lead her astray, she trusted this new animal meant her no harm and continued toward the water, but when the fluffy head with huge black eyes snaked down toward her, she hesitated.

Hello. I'm Daisy, and I was told this is a friendly place where cats can find shelter. I'm extremely thirsty, and hope you don't mind if I drink from your trough.

Welcome, Daisy. I'm Elliott. I'm a guardian llama, and my job is to keep the goats safe from predators, but I watch over the cats, too, whenever I can. I'll walk with you to the water to make sure you aren't bothered while you quench your thirst.

Daisy covered the rest of the distance beside the llama, then jumped up onto the edge of the huge tank. Carefully balancing her wide belly, she crouched to lap the cool water while a donkey watched her from the shade of the barn. Once she drank her fill, she'd be headed for that shade herself. It looked like a good place to rest.

No, it would be better if she stayed on task. No resting until she got inside and found a place to nest. Her kittens weren't going to wait much longer before they burst into the world.

She glanced up at the second story of the barn, where Tony said there would be food waiting. Yes, that's where she'd go next. Hopping down from the edge of the tank, she started to the right, but the llama stopped her.

If you're looking for the food, I can show you the way.

Thank you.

He led her around the building to a fence post driven into the ground right alongside the barn's wall. *The entrance can't be seen from the ground. You have to hop up on here, then climb to the hole. It's easy to find once you're up there.*

Getting to the top of the post wasn't easy, and neither was scaling the wall to where she found a nice, cat-sized space between two logs, but she made it, and was soon entering the cool darkness of the old building.

Welcome. I'm Zak.

She stayed very still until her eyes adjusted and she could see the large tabby perched close by. *I'm Daisy.*

I know. Tony let me know you were on your way. Come, and I'll show you the easiest route to where many others have nested.

Is there anyone else there now?

No, none of our residents make kittens anymore.

Well, that was certainly odd, but she had neither the time nor the inclination to ask him why. She simply plodded in his wake. The route was convoluted but well-worn, and one she'd have no trouble figuring out for herself when she had to come and go later.

Zak landed on the wooden floor and waited for her to catch up. *This is the tack room, where saddles and stuff get stored, and people come in and out of here once in a while.* From there he led her to several stalls bedded with deep straw. *This is mostly where kittens were born back in the day. You can explore later to find the perfect spot, but right now I'll take you to the food, and then show you how to get back out to the water.*

I'll be able to find my way back out.

We never go out the way you came in. Predators wait there sometimes, right up against the wall, where it's hard to see them from high up. Come, I'll show you the safer routes. But first you need to eat.

Yes, she did. And when he took her to the loft, in spite of the weighty scents of dust and hay, the heavenly smell of kibble wafted over her long before they reached the big barrel where the food came out the bottom.

It's an endless supply, so eat all you like.

Daisy needed no further urging, and although she was aware of being watched by many cats, she inhaled a vast amount of food in a short time. Chewing wasn't required.

Once she couldn't squeeze in another piece of kibble, Daisy sat back to have a wash, and wasn't surprised to see cats watching her from various perches. Some were peeking out from behind boxes and buckets piled on one side of the loft, others from up high in the hay.

She eyed the stack of bales, wishing she could

have her babies there, nice and close to the food, but it would be a big risk to birth them where a tom could easily pick up the scent. The memory of when she made that mistake many litters ago still sent a shudder through her. It had been a hard and horrible lesson.

Days ago, Tony told her about the safe places for nesting where horses used to sleep, so that was where she'd birth her kittens. She held her breath when a light contraction gripped her, and released. The kittens were getting into position. It wouldn't be long now.

How do I get to the water from here?

This way. Zak showed her the place where she could work her way down to a fence rail she could walk along to get closer to the trough. *Elliott and Dickens do a good job of patrolling this area near the water, but you still have to keep an eye open for predators.*

I met Elliott. Who is Dickens?

The donkey. There are also horses and cows living out in the fields, and they come here to drink, but they won't bother you. A few of them like cats and can be helpful, but some are big, clumsy oafs, more likely to step on you as not, so you need to take care if you're walking among them.

What about dogs? Tony had said there would be none to bother her, but she still had to ask, because she'd learned they could be as deadly as the coyotes hunting the barnyards at night.

There used to be a couple. But the people moved away after the house burned, and took the dogs with them.

No humans live here, either?
Nope.

How odd. *How does the kibble not run out?*

There's a lady who looks out for us. She's going to live here one day, when she finishes fixing up the house that had the fire, but she says she's a slow builder, so it could be awhile. For now she visits with the cats, tops up the barrel, brushes Dickens and the horses, and gives Elliott and the goats special treats. In the winter she puts big, round bales—from the stack in the barnyard—out for the other animals. And a couple of months ago she made a special place in the machine shed for cats to stay warm in the winter. She put a thing called a pellet stove in there, and it burns all the time.

A haven, Tony had said, and he wasn't wrong. Her muscles clenched again as the kittens continued to shift. She hoped they didn't come for a day or two, until she'd had a few more meals to build up her strength. After she had another drink of water, she checked out the stalls, found a couple of good nests, and curled up in one to have a nice, long nap.

When the sound of an engine woke her up, she stayed very still. Well, as still as she could make herself while her unborn kittens frolicked around, kicking her innards. When the engine shut off, there was general mayhem. The thuds of cats landing, tiny meows and trills, and scampering feet were instantly drowned out by the braying of the donkey—a sound she heard long ago, when she was a tiny kitten, before she was taken from her mother.

Then there was the most wonderful sound of a

lady laughing...

...and something prickled at the back of Daisy's neck just before the door swung open and light flooded the alley between the stalls. Footsteps came closer. Stopped. Then there was a weird sound, and when Daisy went out to investigate, she saw a person climbing a ladder that went through a hole in the ceiling.

Curiosity—and something else she couldn't quite put her finger on—drove her to take the route she learned that morning, and make her way to the loft.

The scene that greeted her was chaotic. The lady was sitting on a bale near the feeder, and there were what seemed like hundreds of cats milling around her, climbing on her, and rubbing against her, and the volume of the purring was crazy.

The lady rubbed heads and ears and petted all the cats, talking to them in a quiet voice that sent shivers up and down Daisy's back.

And then the lady looked up. Went still.

"Well, hello," she said, and held out a hand. "Why don't you come and join us, pretty lady? I have a soft spot for panthers."

Daisy stayed sitting where she was, with her instincts screaming at her. She didn't know what to do. What to believe.

And suddenly, there was a large tabby with one crumpled ear sitting beside her. She blinked, and his image faded just a bit. *Tony?*

Trust yourself, Daisy. This is your best day ever.

So it's true?

CATS

And then some. She's come through a very rough time, and deserves this. Go to her.

Will you come with me?

If you like.

With Tony at her side, she approached, and when the crowd of cats parted to make a path wide enough for one, that's when he stopped. *I'll stay here. You go, Daisy, and show her, so she knows.*

Thank you, Tony. You're more than a guardian, you're an angel, and I will never, ever forget what you've given me.

His image faded, and Daisy continued her journey.

"Oh, my, you have a tummy full of kittens, and you've come at just the right time. I have a wonderful special place for you to give birth, little one, and then we'll get you all fixed up."

Not at all surprised the lady was going to care for her, Daisy did the one thing she could to say thank-you. She lifted her tail straight up, and a small gasp came from the lady, followed by a single word.

"Daisy?"

With the double crook in her tail proudly displayed, she rubbed against the outstretched hand and purred for the lady who once rescued a tiny black kitten from a box in a parking lot.

~~~

CATS: VOLUME ONE
PREVIEW

1

PRINCESS

STRANGE new scents bombarded Princess while she peered out from under the gnarled stump where she'd taken shelter in the night. She blinked. It hadn't been a nightmare. She really *had* been yanked from her bed, stuffed in a box, and taken for a ride in the car.

Then tossed out alongside a highway.

The deafening noise of trucks and cars, and the box shifting with the wind of each passing vehicle, had been real. As had the blinding flashes of light when she finally ripped her way out of the prison they left her in. Claws on fire and gums bleeding, she fled blindly toward the darkness at the side of the road, racing—as though guided by an invisible hand—to this tiny sanctuary where she hid, panting, heart pounding, and petrified. Hours of silence and terror had been punctuated by the sounds of other creatures not far away.

In daylight, things were only slightly less frightening, and a shiver ran through her while she tried to make sense of what she saw. This place wasn't like anything she'd ever seen before. It was the outdoors, where she'd never been allowed to go, but it was different from her yard. The ground felt very curious compared to the miles of grass she remembered tickling her toes on the day she sneaked outside to visit with a handsome cat singing the song of her people.

He asked her to dance and she'd been flattered. Batted her eyelashes and never thought about how the dancing might make her feel. She had no mother to explain there would be a price for a day's freedom. But she'd been driven. Couldn't help herself, and now her humans hated her.

They hadn't put it in words, but there had been sharp looks, and after what they did last night, she could assume nothing else.

Princess shuddered, and shook off the sadness. She had things to do, although she wasn't sure what. And how could that be? How did she know to follow the scents to this place she now timidly surveyed?

Drawn by the irresistible presence of water, she carefully approached the wide silver dish, and wasted little time sniffing and tasting before crouching low to lap with vigor—to fill the emptiness in her belly.

Catching a faint whiff of food, she tossed caution aside to nose through a vast array of scattered dishes, but they were all empty save for a bit of crusting at the edge of one. She made short work of the miniscule offering before something else caught her attention.

Over by the trunk of a wide tree. Wasn't that a ratty toy like the one she had at home? *Oh, dear, how will I ever find my way home to my toys, soft bed, and food dishes? What am I to do?*

A bug skittered across her path, and without thought, she pounced on it. Crunched hungrily. And a vile taste filled her mouth. She shook her head, pawed at her mouth and drool dripped until the bitterness eased.

Best you don't try another of those. They're not meant for eating.

What? Who? She quickly swiveled around, trying to find the source of the voice, but saw no one. She backed toward the safety of her hollow. Or that's what she *thought* she was doing, but miscalculation had her hopping forward when her bottom made contact with something hard. She spun. It was the heavy tunnel thing she'd seen earlier, and inside, another muddy toy.

Want to read the rest of this adventure?
CATS, Volume 1, is available in print and
eBook.
Links at kathrynjane.com

.

CATS: VOLUME TWO
PREVIEW

1

MISTY

Misty, a kitten barely twelve weeks old, left her brothers partially hidden by a bush while she stalked a fat pigeon pecking at grain between railroad ties.

An empty belly her only concern, Misty was out in the open and the lessons her mama drilled into her were little more than a whisper in the back of her mind.

Hunger gave her tunnel vision, and she was bellied down like a seasoned hunter, prepared to take a creature almost double her size. Her heart pounded as though too big for her insides, and her toes vibrated with the need to spring.

She crept a bit closer, locked onto her target, and shifting weight back and forth in preparation for takeoff, her butt wiggled. One breath in, one out, another in— and she soared through the air, stretching her front legs out as far as they would go, and spreading her tiny claws.

Just when they should have sunk into shiny gray feathers, something rammed into her, scraped down her back, and knocked her to the ground.

Run! someone shouted. And without a thought, she burst free of the mass of feathers and raced for the low bush where her brothers were huddled.

Eyes wide, Misty goggled at the enormous hawk standing on the tracks, right where she'd gathered to leap.

The urge to turn and flee deeper into the forest warred with her conscience. She had her brothers to think of. They weren't very brave, and she promised her mama she'd watch out for them. Should she make a run for it so the hawk wouldn't see the boys? *Oh, Mama, help us!*

You're doing fine, Misty. That surely wasn't her mama's voice. No, in fact, it sounded like the one shouting at her to run a minute ago.

Who? She darted a glance around, but couldn't find the speaker.

I'm Sailor.

Where…?

Want to know more about Misty's adventure?
CATS, Volume 2, is available in print and eBook.
Links at kathrynjane.com

ABOUT THE AUTHOR

Rescuing cats has been a lifelong endeavor for Kathryn Jane. It began at the age of five, when a neighbor told her he would have to drown the kittens she'd been playing with if nobody wanted them. She promptly gathered them up and took them home, but her father and the family dog said no dice and they had to be returned.

At seven, having learned the hard way, when Kat found a stray kitten in the warehouse behind where she lived, she left her there, but made a soft bed and took food to her every day. But alas, the dog and dad intervened again, but this time at least, a good home was found with her cousins and the kitten grew old with a wonderful family to care for her.

At sixteen, again, Kat smuggled a kitten into the house, but this time, she got to keep it, and has never been without at least one cat in her home since.

When Kathryn began writing mystery and romance novels, it wasn't surprising when a cat or two spiced up the adventures, and it seemed only natural that after watching TinyKittens ferals online, new ideas for stories were born.

Born also was the desire to help, which is why *proceeds from the print version of the first book, CATS, Volume #1* will go to the TinyKittens Society of BC, Canada. (see details on the website. kathrynjane.com)

80958006R00059

Made in the USA
Columbia, SC
14 November 2017